Ita Margaret Hutchinson O'Croly, Ita Margaret Hutchinson O'Croly

Eastern Echoes with Western Ideas

Vol. 1

Ita Margaret Hutchinson O'Croly, Ita Margaret Hutchinson O'Croly

Eastern Echoes with Western Ideas
Vol. 1

ISBN/EAN: 9783743417120

Manufactured in Europe, USA, Canada, Australia, Japa

Cover: Foto ©Andreas Hilbeck / pixelio.de

Manufactured and distributed by brebook publishing software
(www.brebook.com)

Ita Margaret Hutchinson O'Croly, Ita Margaret Hutchinson O'Croly

Eastern Echoes with Western Ideas

EASTERN ECHOES

WITH

WESTERN ID

VOL. I.

BY

ITA (MARGARET) HUTCHINSON

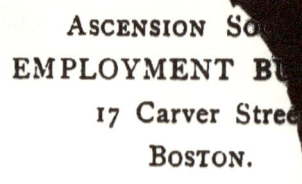

ASCENSION SO
EMPLOYMENT B
17 Carver Stree
BOSTON.

———————

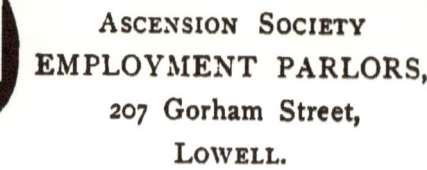

ASCENSION SOCIETY
EMPLOYMENT PARLORS,
207 Gorham Street,
LOWELL.

PREFACE.

The collection of poems embraced in this volume is intended by the author to promote the work of the Ascension Society, a charitable organization that knows neither race nor creed. The first home of the Society in this country was opened in Boston, and it is proposed to open a country branch at South Lowell, where land for the purpose has been purchased by the Society, and it is intended that work upon the erection of the needed buildings will soon be begun. Meantime an office, similar to the one in Boston, will be maintained at 207 Gorham street, Lowell, for the purpose of supplying needy but well-trained domestics with suitable places of employment — a work which has already received much encouragement from the charitably disposed.

Contemporary with the writing of the poem "Mount Melleray," is the founding in 1887 of The Ascension Society at Willmount Castle, where her native land seemed too small a field for the inspiration of the authoress of Eastern Echoes. Her various travels abroad — her experience with school-mates of many nations — forced the school girl, on returning from the scenes (Paris) of art and war to decide on following in the footsteps of Miss Nano Neagle, who also left the French capital only to better if possible the condition of her sex in her native land. The authoress, on the death of an uncle, found her pecuniary circumstances somewhat improved. She dismissed the pupils who gathered round her in her elegant home, and while continuing her work as writer, also set out for a broader field of labor — Boston.

On the 17th of December, 1891, after consulting as to the location, Boston was chosen as the best fitted to be the first home of the young Society on this coast. It has now within its scope no less than 5000 working women of every age, representing many nations and perhaps as many creeds. Every temporary difficulty or emergency in which one of the gentler sex finds herself, comes within the scope of work carried on by The Ascension Society (with three exceptions — theft, present intemperance, or prostitution.) It has two houses in Boston in active work, consisting of Employment Bureau, Temporary Infant Asylum Boarding House, and Free Beds and Board for Poor and Homeless Women and Children.

The Ascension Society houses, 17 and 19 Carver street, Boston, as also the Business house, for several years at 3 Park Square, have been almost continually filled by parties sent for assistance from various Catholic as well as Protestant clergymen. Situations are supplied, and often food and clothing furnished to the needy, without charge, while about 3000 of the leading domestics pay the ordinary price for board, as they occasionally visit the Society on changing their mistresses, which is becoming rather frequent, owing to the custom of residing in a country hotel in summer, while in winter they usually keep help.

C. L. McCleery.

INDEX.

POETICAL PREFACE.

BY THE AUTHOR.

In Baden's Bride we surely see
  The victim of fair love,
The power of earnest prayer
  Sent to the throne above ;
And charity's highest reward
  Has saved an erring soul,
While repentance, broken hearted,
  Brought it to its goal.

Mount Melleray, the Trappist's home
  In Knockmelldown's vale,
Is noted for its pilgrim hordes,
  From every hill and dale.
There silence and obedience great
  Are practiced without pain.

Nocturnal vigils ever kept
   The heavenly land to gain.

The expected and rejected
   Of David's royal line,
Whom jealous fears made Herod seek
   To end that life divine,
Was born of Virgin pure and fair,
   At midnight in a cave,
While hovering angels vied to view
   What Simeon did crave.

The legend of Mount Melleray
   Is but an old man's tale;
It may be true that Mary came
   To mark that rustic vale,
(As fitting place to love, adore,
   And serve her only Son.)
But all men lie, thus David said,
   Beneath the rising sun.

The lost Rosary is mere fact,
   And not a childish boast,
For never did the travelers hope
   To see another coast.

The storm was raging loud and long
  When Raphael, ne'er beguiled,
His client's earnest, hopeful prayer,
  O'er which the nun but smiled.

She soon beheld the billows cease,
  · All dangers then were o'er,
When she could see the Seraph who
  Was spoken of before,
The parcel lost to his client brought
  As stood he on the floor,
While all astonished saw no key
  To ope the well-locked door.

As travelers in many lands
  Will seek the scenes of fame,
Thus did one eagerly inquire :
  What was the builder's name?
It may be high-wrought fancies
  Of Superstition vain,
But Britons, brave and guileless,
  Its truth will still maintain.

Their simple, fertile fancies bright,
  Will build on mountains grand.

They solid believe foundations are,
  Where others see but sand.
They claim that the Madonna fair,
  On that most awful night,
Obtained the blood-signed contract
  And Satan put to flight.

Their confidence in Mary's po
  They'll never have to rue;
You know the tale of Cana's
  Just say it be not true.
The builder, so the legend sa
  To gain all earthly fame,
The slightest mark of disresp
  Refused to Mary's name.

Poetic have the flowers been,
  That haunt the poet still,
Donated to the Sacred Heart
  A fair one's wish to fill.
They decked with other objects
  A little table there;
They stood not near the image gra
  But 'fore a bridal pair.

From Home and Conscience Time may draw
  Sweet thoughts and meditation,
And glances back at School-mates fair,
  Give hours of recreation.
The Ancient Prophecies now give
  All credit to the men
Who lived in Ireland long ago, .
  And who were sages then.

Queenstown, formerly the Cove,
  Is not forgotten here,
Where Johnny saw his mother last,
  The one he loved so dear.
Blarney has many lovely groves,
  Its tales of mystic lore ;
For those who kiss that famous stone
  Were heard of oft before.

The oldest monument on earth
  Ecbatana can show.
The history of Queen Esther
  My readers all well know.
The Mohammedan respect
  Mary's tomb did show,

For there en masse the soldiers
    Would he not permit to go.

The doctrine of Purgatory,
    Praying to or for the dead,
All will be forced to believe
    Who of Ezekiel read.
Who has not known his history,
    Might go that cave to see,
Which two thousand years had pilgrim
    In the land of Chaldea.

The ravens did detective well
    For villains bold were they
Who sought that saintly hermit,
    And on him hands did lay.
His modest cell's a sanctuary now,
    For structure high and grand,
Whose snow-topped steeple far is seen
    Throughout Helvetian land.

The statue that St. Meinrad brought
    Of Mary from his cell
Is in that far-famed snow-capped church
    Within Black Forest dell.

Since the sons of St. Bruno came
　To dwell in that lone vale,
Mary favors great has given—
　Thus runs the Pilgrim's tale.

The Scenes of Winthrop, very near—
　Who's heard not of the tea
Which overtaxed Bostonians
　Just cast into the sea.
It will remind our secretary,
　Who dwells beside that coast,
That of her newly-chosen home
　Poetic lines can boast.

The humble Northumbrian King,
　Whose feast does poet share,
Whose noble life was sacrificed
　His subjects' war to spare.
Tradition is a faithful book,
　We'll cast it not away,
It says St. Oswin's right hand
　Will mould not in the clay.

Tho' wars and revolutions great
　Oft caused poetic lays,

The hand of famed St. Oswin
　Is high in poet's praise.
'Tis said that far away in France
　It dwells in church of fame,
'Tis kept there guarded zealously
　By monks we cannot name.

The Ascension Society
　Will speak to hearts forever,
While my thoughts from my Missing Poems
　I can't and will not sever.
We end the lines with message brought
　To Judea's distant shore,
To King David's royal daughter,
　Whom we'll love for evermore.

Yet Little Gains may finish up,
　The perfect is worth gold,
And "trifles make perfection,"
　Said Pericles of old.
These Little Gains of Lenten days
　Which angels oft will count,
Were practiced in Mosaic times,
　Upon Sinai's mount.

Feast of the Presentation, Boston, Nov. 1896.

BADEN'S BRIDE.

By the mighty Danube River
  Large forests bloom to-day,
All nature there has oft combined
  To make life bright and gay,
That densely crowded thicket,
  The rocks, the shrubs, the trees,
Have made one forest pathless
  For all but birds and bees.

A grand and stately castle now
  Peeps o'er the highest tree,
It holds one noble captive there
  Whom death shall shortly free.
A lady from a distant land,
  An aged father's pride,
A stranger sought to win her hand,
  She soon became his bride.

Nurtured in virtue's stronghold,
　　A convent school of Spain,
Her heart was pure and guileless
　　For life's sunshine or rain.
That she became a robber's bride,
　　A youth in beauty's bloom,
That she shall drink life's bitter gall,
　　They ne'er shall know at home.

In the castle's highest chamber,
　　How many hours each day,
And even in midnight stillness,
　　She'd kneel and for him pray?
For oft in Scripture are we told
　　That God our cry will hear
If we but truly trust in him
　　And still more persevere.

A traveller one day, weather-bound,
　　Knocked at the castle gate,
And demanded hospitality,
　　Because the hour was late.

The lady there received him,
  And then began to weep,
She hastened to her chamber,
  To pray instead of sleep.

That placid face, that humble mien,
  Showed more than simple man,
But she to save that noble life,
  Early that eve did plan.
A faithful porter she besought,
  The priest to well conceal,
And not once tell his whereabouts,
  Till she should it reveal.

This command was scarcely given,
  Than open flew the door,
Her mighty lord, the robber,
  Made up the number four.
He saw at once his consort's face,
  And to dispel her fear,
Kindly demands the stranger's name,
  And how he had come here.

The dinner o'er, that evening late,
    They talk the hours away.
How little did the robber know
    He should not see next day.
By questions great and many, too,
    Who should God's mercy gain,
That sinner shows repentance true,
    His tears will grace obtain.

" Father I've been a wayward man,
    Could I but mercy share,
Those goods and gold I would restore,
    If God will but me spare."
" My child, God's mercy has no bounds,
    Thy faults are not so great
But God thy pardon can now grant,
    You know the good thief's fate."

The robber bent his knee to earth,
    And ere he went to sleep,
Confession made with broken heart,
    To life's end did he weep.

His wife throughout that lonely night,
  Prostrate at Mary's feet,
Could she but see the vision which
  That holy priest does greet.·

Her youthful cries ere dawn are heard,
  She knows not of the grace
Bestowed on him for whom she prayed,
  Ere he did judgment face.
The priest he tried, and not in vain,
  To calm her every fear,
For he a midnight vision had,
  And told what did appear.

" Sleep had scarce hovered round my bed,
  Than I did satan hear,
Demand that soul for wicked deeds,
  Which weigh the balance there,
But his good angel standing by
  His own tale had not told
The sorrow of that erring heart,
  This moment did unfold."

"A handkerchief well wet with tears,
  He in the scales then threw,
That soul in spotless purity
  Towards its maker flew."
Then straight-way to his chamber now
  They went with trembling feet,
They sought and found the handkerchief,
  Well wet beside the sheet.

That body's cold and still in death,
  That face is placid now,
To-day, through fervent, constant prayer,
  A crown doth deck that brow,
For aid was sought through Mary,
  The prayer was not in vain,
Contrition she for him did get
  And that did bliss obtain.

A constant prayer for Mary's aid,
  Will ever bring some grace,
Though we may make no rules of ours,
  Nor name a time or place.

When favors we demand are held
  For some far distant day,
Remember her maternal care
  Is never far away.

The ivy o'er that castle grows,
  The traveller hears the tale,
Where is the bride? has oft been said,
  That dwelt in Baden's vale.
The stolen goods she did restore,
  In convent she does dwell,
In gratitude her days she spends
  Within her lowly cell.

MOUNT MELLERAY.

The golden tints o'er yonder hills,
    Reflect their shadows here,
It must be Melleray's famous mount—
    I fancy it is near.

But beauty oft the heart may lure,
    To scenes in distant lands,
And feelings, too, may changeful prove,
    As ocean's waves or sands.

What solemn chant now mingles with
    The organ peals so clear,
Then can that band angelic be
    Or human that we hear.

No dream but grand reality,
    Saint Bernard's sons are there,
Be still my soul and hearken for
    Thou shalt not long be near.

We shall listen to the voices,
　　Tho' no earthly forms we see,
Hark ! 'tis the Virgin's hymn of praise,
　　First chanted in Judea.

Saint Bernard's rules are rigid,
　　Jew, Pagan, Hottentot,
May tread these far-famed cloisters,
　　But woman's footsteps not.

Alas ! that weaker mortals
　　May here not find a rest,
For woman's feet may never dwell
　　On this lone mountain's breast.

Tho' oft I've been in other lands,
　　No place does seem so fair,
For Melleray's Mount is sanctified,
　　By labor, love and prayer.

'Mid stern grandeur, wooded vales,
　　Hill-tops, oft crowned with snow,
'Mid Summer's sun and Winter's rain,
　　Will Pilgrims come and go.

The organ now has slowly ceased,
  The Vespers hymn is sung,
We may not hear that chant again,
  God's holy will be done.

In silence long, in prayer and toil,
  In fasts and penance sore,
The Trappists spend their strength away,
  Can God's dear Saint do more?

Their noblest deeds of charity
  Time only can reveal,
For conscience highest motives oft
  Will virtue long conceal.

Salvation's powerful emblem there
  Just shows the cold green sod,
Where humble and uncoffined lay
  The honored priests of God.

Man's works are great and many,
  With God's compare them not,
For awe o'erwhelms the creature
  In Melleray's hallowed spot.

Scarce has the sun withdrawn his light,
 To shine on nations west,
Than Compline said, the Trappist monk
 Will take his scanty rest.

The very air is still as death,
 The birds are mute all round,
Nature's day its course has run,
 And silence reigns profound.

Within a poor and lowly cell
 His weary limbs will rest,
Another day is catalogued
 In God's eternal breast.

Two hours from midnight have but flown,
 When 'tis another day,
The matins' bell is calling
 The holy monks to pray.

A long and narrow window there,
 With its uplifted screen,
Revealed but just the merest glimpse,
 Oh, what a solemn scene.

In upright posture, robed in white,
    That band resplendent shine,
While many sinning mortals then
    On sleeping couch recline.

At four in early morning
    They holy Mass begin,
Great blessings to implore for us,
    Or satisfy for sin.

The sterile vale by Knockmeldown,
    To-day a fertile land,
Was made an early harvest ground
    By those whom love command.

The humble monks in hooded gown,
    Their Abbot's words obey,
And silently, with downcast eyes,
    They pass you on the way.

The echo of a Trappist's voice
    The hills can ne'er resound,
For in that lonely wooded dell
    But pick and crowbar sound.

Fate is the mistress grim and stern
  Of many souls who roam,
And happy those, and favored, who
  Find Melleray their home.

Where could a ship be built on earth,
  Or sent by steam or wind,
To any scenes one-half so dear
  As those we leave behind?

Farewell! farewell! Oh, angels bright,
  Bring news to distant shore
Of Melleray, that home of prayer,
  We may not see it more.

Ere Autumn leaves have fallen
  In other lands we'll stray,
By Massachusetts' snowy hills,
  One thousand leagues away.

THE MESSIAH'S COMING.

When man laid down his wearied limbs
　　That winter's night to rest,
When shepherds kept their little flocks
　　Upon the mountain's breast,
When Joseph worn by seeking
　　A shelter for the night,
The signal by the prophets told
　　Eastward had given light.

Silence reigns on earth below,
　　The angels sing on high,
When Mary first is homeless
　　Beneath that starry sky,
When signs that had been written
　　Appeared in deed and word,
In a stable near a manger
　　Was born Christ our Lord.

When man was absent from the scene
   Which angels vie to guard,
When Herod's mighty wrath would strive
   The works of God retard,
When all was utter stillness, then
   Within that lonely cave,
Mary, with a silent heart,
   God to his creatures gave.

The souls that live in turmoil
   And strive, from day to day,
To spend in hoarding earthly gain
   Life's useful hours away,
Should build within the secret caves
   Of their own throbbing heart
A silent and most spotless crib,
   Whence God would ne'er depart.

LEGEND OF MELLERAY.

When mighty rocks 'mid trees and shrubs
    Had filled the hills and vales
That forms the now most hallowed spot
    Renowned in lengthy tales,
Just when the laws had been repealed
    Of cruel penal days,
Two monks the order of La Trappe
    Through Melleray wend their ways.

One day they leave their cottage there
    To mount the distant hill,—
The aged monk an Abbot is,
    Pale, worn, tired, and ill.
" We'll seek a level, fertile spot,"
    Within their hearts they prayed,
And God doth manifest His will,
    E'er through the mount they strayed.

A mile or very little more
  Their cottage is behind,
Monks, birds, beasts, and all around
  In silence have combined
A homestead for his brethren,
  A site beside that hill,
The only thought except of God,
  The Abbot's heart doth fill.

When lo! a human form they see
  Approach them in the vale,
She begs an alms for God's dear sake,
  Such is the Abbot's tale,
His only wealth for future store,
  A franc he to her gave ;
We are poor alas! good woman,
  'Tis from poverty you crave.

Then turning to his brother monk
  Inspiration sudden came,
Of that female now inquire
  Knowledge of this mount and name.

As quick as passing wind,
  He looked where she had been;
Behold! the virgin now had flown,
  The spot was fair and green.

His staff he left to mark the site
  Where Melleray Abbey stands,
Famous among saintly shrines
  In this and other lands.
Now Mary gets the credit
  Of begging on that day
The only mite the Abbot had
  And did she not repay.

She showed the place the Lord designed
  To be a home of prayer,
'Twas barren then, 'tis fertile now,
  Growing daily green and fair;
Youth in its schools a haven find
  A home of sanctity and lore,
While daily crowds of pilgrims come
  From many a distant shore.

THE LOST ROSARY.

THE LOST ROSARY.

In the far famed city of Liege
  A chosen spot indeed,
For God has nurtured in its breast
  Great saints in hours of need—
In Rue de Chateau there
  A stately convent stands,
The early home of ladies
  From many distant lands.

And when school days are over
  Each pupil seeks her home,
Perchance a nun is with her,
  To cross the raging foam.
Two children left one morning there
  To reach old England's shore,
One prayed for Raphael's guidance
  As oft she did before.

The slow train reached the Antwerp port,
    The distant sea looked mild,
But long ere land had disappeared
    The ocean's waves grew wild.
The northern waters furiously
    The steamer's side were beating,
While loudly claimed the sailors
    The compass must be cheating.

The captain now and then declared
    That she was going right,
For should we have gone northward
    He'd have seen the northern light;
The Cattegat and Skager Rack
    Were dreaded on that day,
While almost lifeless bodies
    Then around the vessel lay.

The nun o'er her protegee watched
    With almost maternal care,
And she besought the ocean's Star
    The dying one to spare;

That prayer was scarcely ended
  Than that feeble form there
With more than childlike confidence
  Spoke of that passing prayer.

Scarce had the sister reached her bed
  Than the feeble form did say:
" Sister, we'll all safe arrive.
  To Raphael I did pray
E'er we left the convent chapel,
  When we made our visit there.
Our life, our baggage, books and all
  I've asked great Raphael's care."

Overcome for the moment
  By the faith of the child,
She ne'er expressed a word
  But turned off and smiled,
When suddenly the billows
  Did in the distance stay,
Immediately the harbor reached
  The ship did anchor weigh.

That almost doomed vessel
   With all its living freight
Was catalogued as lost,
   But it was only late ;
The train was quickly boarded
   And its door wide opened flew
When it reached the nearest depot
   Where it had long been due.

A dark-haired youth with brilliant eyes
   His client came to cheer,
A tiny parcel brought he too
   And then did disappear.

The nun in consternation asks
   Her pupil for his name,
As the donor of that parcel
   She would not know again :
" He brought me here my Rosary,
   I've seen him not before,
You know I am a stranger
   Upon this foreign shore."

The receiver of the Rosary
  Whom death sought to demand,
Then held her little treasure
  Within her tiny hand
And says: when e'er we journey far,
  Let us to Raphael pray,
For he our parcels lost will bring
  However long the way.

HOME.

Home, what art thou not to mortal here,
  Where e'er on earth his lot is cast.
The sweetest sound to human ear,
  The word it prizes first and last.

Home scenes of early childhood,
  Where we together played;
Home, native land and cherished too,
  Where older folks have stayed.

Home, the parting from thy shores
  More lonely seems to me,
To-day, beneath a foreign flag,
  Than when I've turned from thee.

Turned towards a western land
  Where mighty rivers flow,

Where man may reach a higher goal,
   Where all things onward go.

But 'tis not home, that dear old spot
   Where we all dwelt of old,
The shamrock here ne'er decks our path,
   But can be bought for gold.

The new is well, yes for a while,
   But Oh! give me the old,
For parents and a native land
   May ne'er be bought for gold.

Home, be it a lordly mansion grand,
   Or a poor peasant's cot,
It satisfies the human heart,
   Its features matter not.

When cold and harsh imperious words
   Of strangers greet our ears,
They oft recall our native home,
   As do they bygone years.

Home! however poor or simple,
  Thy memory shall have part
For ages and for ever still,
  Within the human heart.

Home, seat of faithful friendships,
  Tho' thy treasures be but few,
Thy grandest and thy greatest gifts
  Were friends both tried and true.

What like that sweet maternal voice,
  Which may be still to-day —
Which warned us in wayward hours
  Of dangers far away.

Compare that grand paternal care
  With that of new made-friends,
When dismal looks the coming cloud,
  The latter's interest ends.

Give me a playmate sister,
  Or brother young and bold,

Their memory softens bitter hours
  Among the strangers cold.

Home ! in dreams I oft revisit thee,
  And wake in deep emotion,
Alas ! to find I am not there
  But far beyond the ocean.

Should fate decree that I may leave
  This new-made land to roam,
May it decree that I in thee
  May dwell, my native home.

Home — fare thee well — tho' many miles
  Thou' art across the main,
May heaven grant 'twill be my lot
  To see thy shores again.

Home — my long buried treasure,
  The noble, king or slave,
Could never find a dearer tomb,
  My throbbing heart's its grave.

GLIMPSES OF SCHOOL-MATES.

GLIMPSES OF SCHOOL-MATES.

How many bright tho' tearful eyes
  In dreams I sadly see
From the Athens of Old Ireland,
  That city on the Lee.

From the mansions of famed Limerick,
  How many young and small,
Do some companions cherish,
  But are sisters unto all.

And old historic Cashel
  Is not forgotten here,
Its children long the faith have spread
  In regions far and near.

And one is in Mohammed's land,
  In mortal dread each day,

To speak and act as christian should,
　To fast, to watch and pray.

The burning sun o'er Hindostan
　May scarcely ever rise,
Except o'er heads of school-mates dear,
　Whose very names we prize.

The land of famed Columbus,
　With its noted Fundy Bay,
Has attracted my companions dear,
　To its regions far away.

In British North America,
　Where prowls the grizzly bear,
Some teach the savage Indians
　Who roam that frozen sphere.

And by the ice bound Frazer
　Have dwelt for many a year,
A few of those fond school-mates:
　They aid the black-robed there.

By the mighty Guadalquiver,
  In the sunny land of Spain,
Some have followed Saint Theresa,
  They we may not meet again.

' Neath the clear blue sky of Paris
  Have some long since made their home,
And to the distant missions westward,
  They may yet have cause to roam.

But others still are farther gone
  To Australia's distant shore,
They teach the aborigines
  The one God to adore.

Oft did I wish to share their fate,
  Upon that sunny shore ;
But Providence has destined me
  For harder works and more.

The romance of early mission life
  Was not my lot to share,

But the densely populated towns
  Whose snares for souls I fear.

Alas! the dream is over,
  My school-mates all are gone;
The brilliant beams of summer sun
  Right in the window shone.

Why should that glimpse of nations
  Be nothing but a dream?
The morrow's sun will prove it so,
  'Twill pass with life's great stream.

Farewell my distant school-mates,
  For we may meet no more,
'Till nations rise to judgment,
  Upon the eternal shore.

And few among the cherished ones,
  My very class-mates dear,
Have stayed within that lonely dell,
  The world to roam they fear.

How oft in grand processions now,
  I muse on those there,
When we in veiled splendor
  Have listened to that prayer.

That God would watch and cherish
  The distant ones and near,
Who learned from the Brigitines
  His will to love and fear.

Were we dwelling in the frozen north,
  Or ' neath the tropic rays,
We'll think of thee Saint Brigids,
  And happy youthful days.

POETIC FLOWERS,

DEDICATED TO

MRS. THOMAS F. GALVIN,

BROOKLINE, MASS.

A cool clear breeze that summer's eve
  The leaves and flowers did part,
While ' neath the florist's dome that night,
  Re-echoed Sacred Heart.

His lady's voice, a sonorous one,
  Maternally and sweet,
Just named through inspiration grand,
  The words that saints would greet.

Give to my friend, she softly said,
  Just as we stood to part,
A box of fresh and choice flowers,
  Give for the Sacred Heart.

The florist was of Martha's School,
  And said beneath that dome :
Heed not my wife, the church has much,
  But take these to your home.

The mingled voices of his men,
  The scent of plant and flower
Enhanced that scene on Tremont Street,
  That mid-eve summer's hour.

That scene so calm, those flowers so grand,
  In poetic dreams had part,
And ere the morning sun did shine,
  They decked the Sacred Heart.

In Notre Dame Des Victoires Church,
  An altar set apart
Was perfumed by those fresh-blown flowers,
  Close to the Sacred Heart.

Oh! creatures learn a lesson grand,
  Of each day give a part,

In spirit, if no more you can,
    Give to the Sacred Heart.

Take not a leave of Martha's book,
    Mary chose the better part,
For it she was commended high,
    And by the Sacred Heart.

Those flowers were used as friendship's gift,
    Then they decked an altar fair;
But ere the evening sun had set
    There knelt a bridal pair.

How brightest hopes are blasted,
    How intentions go for naught,
Thus mused the flower's receiver,
    As on their use she thought.

The flowers are dead and gone,
    And still the altar there
Recalls the poet's vision,
    Of that good lady fair.

THE UNKNOWN BUILDER,

OR

THE CATHEDRAL LEGEND.

THE UNKNOWN BUILDER,

OR

THE CATHEDRAL LEGEND.

In the northwestern part of France,
  Short distance from the shore,
The traveler hears a graphic tale
  Of Satan's craft and lore;
There stands a grand Cathedral
  Whose builder none can name,
Tho' the splendor of its structure
  Has gained undying fame.

The tourist oft is dazzled
  In viewing its lofty spires,
And of his Briton driver guide
  He generally inquires:
How many years this Church has stood
  The tempest and the rain,
And was the high-souled builder found
  Within this fertile plain.

Alas! the simple country folks
    The legend still retain,
The builder of this grand old Church
    A secret shall remain;
Past centuries have seen it stand,
    Tho' the ocean's billows roar
Are heard within its noble aisles,
    That almost bound the shore.

In the dark and Iron Ages
    Of superstitious lore,
There lived a country gentleman
    By this northwestern shore;
He studied witch and wizard craft
    And thus in seeking fame
Through his satanic majesty,
    We may not know his name.

Satan, the leader of the proud,
    Appeared to him one night
Saying: be but mine forever
    And sign this contract right,

Then riches, pleasures, shall be thine
  For many years to come,
But at this hour, on certain date,
  You e'er must share my home.

Upon this poor rejected spot
  You'll rise to earthly fame,
For you may build a Babel Tower
  And it shall bear thy name;
But last of all my enemy
  You never must respect,
For those who honor Mary
  My counsels might reject.

I'll accept your riches, pleasures,
  And sign the contract now,
But disrespect to Mary's name
  Shall darken not my brow;
Well, said His Satanic Majesty,
  Then sign this in your blood,
For her followers have outdone me
  Since Creation and the Flood.

The contract's made, that night is passed,
   The future will bring fame,
For the rapturous tourists ever ask
   What is the builder's name.
Alas! The tale, tho' awful,
   Is heard along that shore,
How he sold himself to Satan,
   Such said the folks of yore.

'Twas midnight, and that dreadful hour
   Seemed dismal on the shore,
Had he that blood-signed contract
   He'd serve his God once more,
But Mary for that contract sought
   And obtained it on that night,
When it declared to darker realms
   With Satan he'd take flight.

He stood alone, all friendless,
   But Mary's aid he sought,
Refugium Peccatorum
   Then comfort to him brought;

The Cathedral bells were tolling
  The midnight hour there
When His Satanic Majesty
  Must meet that lady fair.

The struggle soon was o'er,
  The demon wishes ever ill,
Saying "You broke that blood-signed contract
  While I my part did fill.
You brought me here my enemy
  Whom I ever will disown
But I one satisfaction have
  Thy name shall be unknown."

Mary got that contract then,
  Signed on that direful night,
And she commanded Satan
  To quickly take his flight;
As her client had refused
  Her memory to defame
She would require that deed
  And he was put to shame.

SAINT OSWIN'S REPENTANCE.

SAINT OSWIN'S REPENTANCE.

The Druidal fires had ended scarce
  Along the Saxon shore,
Than Christian kings and nobles
  Were almost steeped in gore.

The kingdom of Northumbria,
  A small tho' rich domain,
Was ruled by youthful pious king
  Who will not it retain.

In Roman martyrology
  We find a Bishop's name,
The chaplain of King Oswin,
  Of more than mortal fame.

Tho' chaplain to the palace,
  Nothing decent he'd retain;

Therefore his kingly master
 His anger can't restrain.

The poor were the receivers
 Of gifts both great and small,
That through the royal orders
 To Aidan's lot would fall.

The foggy mists of England's shore
 Which held the sun's bright rays,
As darkening clouds of even
 Bespeak the close of days.

Saint Aidan to a poor man gave
 His horse, his trap, and all,
.On foot his homeward journey made
 Towards that royal hall.

The king conceived the chaplain's deed
 The nobles looked aghast,
When by the royal palace door
 Saint Aidan calmly passed.

What hast been then my foal's fate,
　My gift this day to thee?
You now must seek my prized horse
　And bring it back to me.

"My lord and king," Saint Aidan said.
　"A soul redeemed by God
Is dearer far to me than foal
　Of mare on yonder sod."

Those words so gently spoken then
　Impressed that royal heart;
That scene, tho' calm, in history's page
　Will ever form a part.

The youthful King took off his crown,
　And pale as corpse in shroud
He, kneeling, pardon humbly asked
　Before that royal crowd.

"My Lord and Bishop," said the King,
　In accent meek and mild,

"I humbly thy forgiveness crave,
  As an imprudent child."

Then turning to the courtiers,
  With eyes well filled with tears,
Saint Aidan softly whispered then
  "He'll never rule us years.

"Of this King we are unworthy,
  I feel it more and more,
For never did I see a Prince
  So humble once before."

The prophecy was proven true,
  Ere many days were o'er,
At festive board they'll never meet
  That saintly King once more.

Northumbria's happy kingdom,
  Had seen its better days,
Its saintly ruler had disdained
  Also the soldier's praise.

Then seeking a companion there
  To journey far away,
He left his crown and kingdom—
  Such did the poets say.

But Oswald, full of treachery,
  Feared that some future day
The loving heart of Oswin then
  Northumbria would sway.

Then money sold that saintly King,
  A follower him betrays,
He is pursued by Oswald's hordes
  Beneath the sun bright rays.

A Martyr King, his title is,
  To save his people war
He forsook his earthly kingdom
  For peaceful lands afar.

But cold and cruel Oswald's heart
  Demands that noble life,

And Oswin's cowardly follower
   Was Judas in the strife.

That deed so coldly perpetrated
   And that peaceful reign o'er,
The fame of saintly Oswin
   Has passed from shore to shore.

For mortification ne'er could touch
   The hand that cast away
The crown of fair Northumbria
   Upon that fatal day.

My readers oft may smile or laugh,
   But the poets simple lay
Was verified in days of yore,
   So English writers say.

TALES OF BLARNEY.

TALES OF BLARNEY.

Tradition says, that long ago,
   In the Cromwellian· days,
Blarney was but a simple dell
   Where now the tourist strays.

A soldiers' guard was ever kept
   Around that castle there
Whose wondrous stone of magic gift
   Is read of far and near.

One evening came a soldier young,
   But drunkard, bold and gay,
To see his wife and only child,
   Such did the legend say.

In drunken fit that soldier then
   His loved ones did not spare,

The morrow brings him consciousness
And with it dwells despair.

Tho' cold and hunger's pangs are felt,
    His wife, both young and fair,
With friend or neighbor never once
  - That woeful tale did share.

Till on that shrill December eve
    That shriek of dread despair,
Betold the awful fatal tale
    Within that cabin there.

That soldier on that dreadful eve,
    As he for whiskey sought,
By accident an instrument
    Death to his loved one brought.

That lovely dying angel girl
    Scarce had six summers seen,
When all beheld that martyred one
    Speak calmly and serene.

" Papa, don't make mamma cry,
  Promise to drink no more,
Be good to mamma when away
  And when you come ashore."

Then those words so long remembered
  Made one heart there feel sore.
Alas! That form is lifeless now,
  And he will drink no more.

One lesson taught that soldier brave,
  But Oh! How dearly bought,
It cost a life, his only child,
  Who his conversion sought.

The lonely mother's heart gave up
  All that she here could love,
But oft she felt her angel child
  Would pray for her above.

A braver, truer, nobler man,
  Ne'er stood within that vale,

He kept his promise faithfully,
  Such is the old folks' tale.

That castle which long stood the breeze,
  Upon Green Erin's shore
Will tower aloft, the tourists say,
  A century or more.

Its stone—that famous Blarney stone—
  Who has not heard its name?
Bravely defied Cromwellian shot,
  Therefrom has come its fame.

The tourist oft of other land
  Will kiss the Blarney Stone,
Where once a daring youthful lad
  To waters 'neath was thrown.

A mother's fond and only son,
  No wealth could e'er atone,
For that lifeless mangled body,
  Where rippling waters moan.

His eighteenth year he never saw,
  That brave, that only son,
That tragic tale, will e'er descend
  ' Till ages course has run.

That river 's ever deep and wide,
  Whose streams from hill and dale
Have wandered through the many groves
  Of Blarney's far famed vale.

That river turns the grand old wheel
  Where Blarney Tweed is made ;
Where Irish-Scotch and English hands
  For work are fully paid.

Mahoney Brothers both have past
  To the eternal shore ;
How often they the wolf did keep
  Far from the poor man's door.

The widow or orphan their aid
  Never once sought in vain ;

Their noblest deeds were quietly done
  In sunshine and in rain.

The warbling birds of Blarney groves,
  The noon-day brilliant rays,
The thundering wheel, the Castle stone,
  Deserve the poet's praise.

There stands a convent, modest, small,
  Within that lovely vale ;
The village church, of recent days,
  Completes the school-boy's tale.

But older folks, of memory great,
  Say ' neath the Shandon Bells,
The genius of Mahoney's race,
  That lifeless writer dwells.

He died, where Charlemagne of old
  Thought fitted to depart ;
But he must needs in Erin rest,
  There ever dwelt his heart.

They brought him there from sunny France,
　His tomb the tourists see,
Beneath the bells by him renowned,
　That sound along the Lea.

The monastery of St. Denis
　Has had his latest days
While few have been the living men
　Who have not heard his lays.

Now with a poet's license great
　I've left that lovely vale,
And on my homeward journey then
　I heard the old man's tale.

"There is a grave, 'tis scarcely green—
　The fever snatched away
That poet monk in early youth,
　There Gerald Griffin lay."

With Christian brother side by side,
　The novice monk there lay,

I've twined the ivy wreath and knelt
　A moment just to pray.

That ivy long must withered be
　But memory seems to say
The poet of the collegians
　Must live in hearts to-day.

Onward by that hill-side grave,
　Much nearer Blarney Vale
My dreams of interest were aroused
　Just by the glowing tale.

You now can look, the old man said,
　The green spot yonder see,
The last home of that Collins brave
　Beside the River Lea.

He sought the Arctic regions far,
　Where white men never trod,
There missionary in future days
　May preach the word of God.

The model of the famed Jeannette
  Now decks that young man's grave,
While on his foul companions' heads
  Justice will vengeance crave.

We left that place and traveled on,
  We soon did reach the vale,
Whose castle high above the trees
  Will end the old man's tale.

When Cromwellian wars were over,
  In lands were soldiers paid,
Then Blarney to an Englishman
  Was given, it is said.

The March winds blew and cold the breeze
  When soldier came to view
The portion for his bravery great
  Was mean, said Jeffrey too.

The land is distant many miles,
  Chaffing his pipe away ;

Said Jeffrey to the soldier there :
     You'll reach it not to-day.

Its people bold and giant·like,
     Act as lions in the fray ;
If life you prize my good young man,
     Go back to Dublin Bay.

Terror-stricken and down-hearted,
     Being tired and footsore,
The English soldier halted, saying :
     I'll travel on no more.

Then take this pipefull with you
     To smoke along the way ;
Tell not the errand foolish, vain,
     Which brought you here to-day.

But I shall not be heartless, friend,
     Yet I can't give you gold ;
Alas, there grand old Blarney then
     For half a crown was sold.

But who can tell that soldier's name,
  It matters not for aught;
Tobacco and a half a crown
  That lovely valley bought.

The sun was slowly setting then
  Behind the distant hill;
When heard I had the old man's tale
  Which does those poems fill.

John Bull could hold the battle-field
  And lay the Irish low,
But mother wit bought Blarney Vale,
  Such does the story go.

But they who centuries long past
  Beguiled the soldier there,
Inherit still sufficient wit
  To cheat the poet fair.

The palm of victory is theirs,
  And will forever more,

For Paddy's right to mother wit
  Is known from shore to shore.

The poet will leave the famed cove
  For far Columbia's shore,
Where Irish wit and Irish hearts
  Will live for ever more.

TIME.

Think only of the present,
  The future may not come,
The past cannot return,
  This moment is thine own.

And ere these lines are written,
  This momeut shall have passed,
To teach the erring mortal
  That nothing here will last.

Just by the sea shore calmly stand,
  Or by a fountain pause,
And think how all must quickly cease
  But nature's changeless laws.

O, Time, thou fleeting shadow,
  Tho' present, ever past,
The tale to all you vainly tell,
  That nothing here shall last.

Time's book can tell over joys and woes,
  The secrets of all ages
Are ever deeply graven there,
  In thy unwritten pages.

When deeds of darkness long ago
  Have passed the minds of men,
Thou oft wilt tell the evil one
  And search life's record then.

The innocent thanksgiving oft
  Have doled to thee and thine,
How many years and days have they
  Been held in doubtful line.

Till thou who metest justice fair,
  Beneath the rising sun,
Hast given the truest sentence
  That ever judge could don.

Time, thou hast shown thy power great,
  In every place and land and clime,

Thou hast crumbled tombs to dust,
   Thou canst end the church bell chime.

Thou art the ever ruling being,
   In foreign lands and home,
Thou hast governed the past
   So thou canst days to come.

Tho' bright may be our prospects here,
   Thou canst life quickly end,
And on that hour, whatever date,
   How many years depend.

If spent thou art but lightly,
   No art can thee restore,
May Heaven grant that here below
   We ne'er misspend one hour.

Go, quickly seize the present,
   It never may return,
And for its moments wasted now,
   Thy only chance is mourn.

MISSING POEMS.

Restore to me my missing leaves,
  Give back my once seen pages,
Their lines my memory might recall,
  Were I among the sages.

Go search my lines in every nook,
  The wealth of days of yore
Has vacant left my memory's hall,
  Where long they've dwelt before.

My missing lines of other days,
  And countries far away,
The gold of memory's brighter years,
  Oh! Give me them to-day.

Return me but the fragments now
  Of my once treasured pages,

They are my childhood's offspring
And not the works of sages.

Go find for me the missing leaves,
   The hopes of future years
May buried be with these lost lines,
   Such are my present fears.

My dreams shall haunt the very spot
   Where once these lines were lost,
The missing ones now seem to me
   The lines I prize the most.

They told of monuments and men,
   Who once arose to fame,
And this knowledge to thy memory
   In recent travels came.

Restore my youthful progeny,
   Oh! Printer seek again,
Thy archives might as yet—perchance
   The missing leaves retain.

The golden thoughts of present hopes
  My grief cannot restrain,
Find but the missing jewels and
  My eyes shall beam again.

These lines were writ of many lands
  And objects of renown,
Restore them to my aching heart,
  'Twill take away my frown.

The poet may travel memory's halls
  Or dwell on foreign shore,
But the brilliant thoughts of other hours
  May now be his no more.

My eyes are dim, the clouds are dark,
  Where brightness ever shone,
In searching for the missing links
  I'll wander forth alone.

How many scenés now far away,
  By distant hill and dale,

Were memorized in missing leaves,
  Such is the poet's tale.

Then find these poems, they're precious,
  Thy recompense is gold,
Bring me but tidings hopeful here,
  Prove they have not been sold.

SAINT MEINRAD'S RAVENS.

In a dark and dismal forest,
  Near by to Mount Atzel,
A young lord of Suabia
  As hermit there did dwell.

The reveried genius of Helvetia
  Found place within that brain,
For the noted Hohenzollern counts
  Formed his ancestral train.

His sanctity and learning brought
  Pilgrims from many lands,
Unnumbered they shall e'er remain
  As ocean's waves or sands.

Alas! that faithful solitary
  Must seek some lonely cell,

Where to commune alone with God,
  He ever more will dwell.

Till the cruel banditti then,
  With hearts both hard and cold,
Dispatched that saintly hermit,
  In hopes to find his gold.

But that angelic spirit had
  Bestowed upon the poor
His earthly all while here below,
  The heavenly banks secure.

But justice now will seek the hands
  Who did that dreadful deed ;
The poor to find the murderers
  With God will intercede.

Two ravens soon the villains bold
  Pursue both night and day,
Till in a grand and ancient church
  They'll soon be held at bay.

The villains close those massive doors,
　To keep outside the foe,
But the ravens by their strategy
　Then through the window go.

All hopes for flight are over,
　The ravens caught their prey.
The banditti then did suffer,
　So the Suabians say.

The croaking raven oft we find
　The hermit's friend before,
My readers all the story heard
　Of Paul, the saint of yore.

The beasts that roam the forest wild,
　And birds that warble there,
How oft they've been the only friend
　The hermit's meal to share.

Back to the days of Charlemagne
　We trace that hermit lord,

Who scarcely adolescent sought
   The forest or the wood.

His vows he made in early youth,
   The abbey of Richneau
Has heard pronounced the sacred words
   Where barefoot pilgrims go.

Some fifty years had passed away,
   Ere Bruno's sons had come
To build around that tragic spot
   The future pilgrim's home.

The church of Einsiedeln,
   With its snow-topped steeple,
Has pilgrim throngs of grand and great,
   Of every land and people.

The sole possession Meinrad brought
   From his lone mountain cell
Was the unpretending image
   Found in that favored dell.

Black is that forest's name to-day,
True color for the deed.
May Meinrad's prayers in heaven
For sinners intercede.

ECBATANA.

The far-famed Ecbatana,
  With its temples overthrown,
In the poet's estimation
  Has grandeur little known.

Its fame in ages past and gone,
  Its royalty and lore,
Its Jewish pilgrims' visits there
  Two thousand years and more.

There the tomb of Esther,
  With its massive door of stone,
By the sword of Tamerlane
  Was surely overthrown.

But Ecbatana can lay claim,
  Tho' kingdoms passed away,

That the restored mausoleum
  Was built where Esther lay.

Tho' Belshazzar's power was great,
  The Medes to it laid claim,
Ecbatana was their capital,
  Which held the tomb of fame.

The conquerors of Belshazzar,
  Who held o'er Persia sway,
,Would find the obscure Hamadan
  The Ecbatana of that day.

The Orontes' beauteous shades,
  Above a thousand streams,
With ruined temples round,
  Still haunt the poet's dreams

The sarcophagi there,
  Covered with granite red,
Will speak not to the living,
  As the language long is dead.

EZEKIEL'S CAVE.

When on our distant journeys
  In the ancient Chaldea,
On the banks of the Chobar,
  Ezekiel's Cave we see.
Its tradition's very simple,
  The saint of visionary lore ;
His tomb was long revisited
  On the bank of famed Chobar.

When the tribes were dispersing,
  The Chaldeans' fears were grave,
And resolved they to destroy
  The pilgrims at the Cave.
A massacre had followed
  Had not the prophet dead,

By the division of the Chobar,
 The enemy mislead.

The superb surrounding edifice
 Has its golden lamp no more,
Tho' the Asiatic Jew
 Will visit as of yore.
The captives sworn in that famed land
 Have long since taken flight,
The stipulated golden lamp
 Burns neither day or night.

That noted Cave of Chaldea,
 Where Ezekiel lay,
Is now a cavern old, decayed
 Of a pre-Christian day ;
And like the tomb of Rachel,
 Went the Israelites there
In pious pilgrimage,
 To offer up a prayer.

CALIPH OMAR'S MAGNANIMITY.

Galistan says of Omar,
  That great caliph of the East,
That when he took Jerusalem,
  He to Bethlehem made haste.

Tho' Mussulman, the caliph knelt
  Where the Messiah was born,
Then visited the Mary's tomb,
  Our Lady Star of Morn.

And to his soldiers gave command
  That none should enter there,
Lest they disturb that sanctuary,
  But one by one for prayer.

Go tell the learned heretic
  How Saladin and Omar,

And the bright lamp of the former,
Honored our Morning Star.

Of the Persian Jews 'tis written
That of Mary's name they spoke
With disrespect to Ali's train—
Such of them Chardin wrote.

The followers of Ali they
Indignant then became,
And would have slain the culprits
Who Mary dared defame.

The Jews then fled that city,
Not one did there remain,
The massacre had been their lot—
Compensation for their pain.

Mahomet honored Mary,
In the Koran is her name,
Among the four just women
Of noted earthly fame.

THE IMMIGRANT'S JOURNEY.

The tugboat's crew is ready,
  The throng is drawing near,
An hour or very little more,
  'Twill sped the ocean there.
Alas! this motley crowd
  Is formed of young and old
Then heed they not the bitter winds
  Of March, both bleak and cold.

Tho' they must come from far and near,
  By steamer, car or train,
They're never late for roll call,
  In sunshine or in rain.
How many broken-hearted ones
  They leave upon the shore,
Perchance on earth to meet again,
  Perhaps to meet no more.

A fond, tho' aged mother there,
  Whose course seems almost run,
With sobbing heart is parting from
  Her all—her only son.
" God bless you now, my darling boy;
  Don't forget your poor old mother,
For well you know, not long ago
  The landlord shot your brother."

In course of years poor Johnny's health
  Gave notice of decay;
The doctors order native air;
  Then Johnny sails away.
'Tis midnight when the oceaner
  Did reach the Queenstown quay;
So he can see his native spot,
  Just by the dawn of day.

The homestead reached ere noonday sun
  Had shed one brilliant ray;
At Johnny's door the ivy grows,
  This cold November day.

My readers, guess the story sad.
    But the dead will tell no tale;
The grave holds all that Johnny seeks
    In yonder sunny vale.

His new-made friends are far away,
    In Montana's silver mines,·
And Johnny's saddening story
    They'll get in tear-blot lines.
"My childhood's home is dreary,
    Where first I saw the day.
My mother's 'neath, the moss-grown sod,
    Now mouldering in the clay.

"That grave has held my father's bones;
    A loved and faithful brother's;
More precious to my heart to-day,
    My fond and cherished mother's."
But ere this tear-stained letter
    Had reached Columbia's shore,
The penman passed to brighter lands,
    Whence he shall write no more.

THE ANNUNCIATION.

When Gabriel descended
  That midnight hour there,
King David's royal daughter
  Humbly knelt in prayer;

He gave that potent message
  As noiselessly he trod
The Virgin's humble chamber,
  The favored one of God.

Then wonderingly she pondered
  On what Gabriel said,
How many prophets had foretold,
  As she that hour had read,

That from the root of Jesse,
  Of David's royal line,

Would one day a Redeemer come,
  Both potent and divine.

Then Mary, notwithstanding
  All that the angel said,
Deferred a moment her consent—
  Such we have oft times read.

The angel, seeing her humble fears
  While on that spot he trod,
Replied in a consoling voice:
  "Thou hast found grace with God."

ANCIENT PROPHECY OF IRELAND

Elbana (Dublin) shall yet be ruined
    Beneath the fire of cannon ;
A warrior fleet shall hover there
    From Blarney to the Shannon.
Such said the great St. Malachy
    With MacAuliffe of Duhallow,
Even the Druidal chiefs
    In the Prophecy do follow.

In years to come ere long,
    So did the sages say,
The children of the Emerald Isle
    The Saxon won't obey.
The land from tyrant thraldom
    Forever shall be free,
And her children long in foreign climes,
    That day will live to see.

The Druid Fionn MacCumhaill
    With all his dreaded lore,
Maintained the same prophetic code
    Regarding Erin's shore.

Its sons shall rule their native land.
  In Columbian prophecies we see
That when the judgment trumpet sounds
  Green Ireland shall not be.

To see the last and awful day,
  Erin's sons at home are spared,
As Ireland ere that hour
  The ocean's bed had shared.
The horrors of the anti-Christ
  Will not their lot then be,
As Erin ere the record day
  Will sink into the sea.

Its sons are true and bold and brave,
  They crave for freedom ever ;
The tests they've stood for ages
  No tortures could them sever.
Undying their love of fatherland,
  Of kindred and of home,
But who can tell their history—
  Fidelity to Rome.

"CONSCIENCE."

Rest and peace a troubled soul
  Had sought in many lands ;
Her hopes on earth, her fears, too,
  Were varied as the sands.

With pen she toiled to leave her thoughts
  Of scenes and life elsewhere,
In castle grand and stately halls,
  But peace she found not there.

No riches great, or learning, too.
  Or scenes in any clime,
Could all combined give peace of heart
  Where Conscience did decline.

With books of sage and poet,
  By mountain and by lake,

She sought to lull that voice to sleep,
  But Conscience would awake.

'Twas dusk, the tapers glimmered
  Before the altar fair ;
No living being was near,
  A presence still was there.

Then silent adoration
  The soul a moment fed,
Peace dwells within that heart
  And tears with joy are shed.

Youthful hours in lands afar,
  Did still that voice a time,
But it would wake uncalled again,
  In every place and clime.

The crowded street or hustling throng
  Could never still its sounds,
Unless the breath of life withdraws,
  That inner voice resounds.

SCENES OF WINTHROP.

DEDICATED TO

MRS. W. P. JOHNSON,

NEE DOWNEY.

———

'Tis noonday, and the summer's sun
  Shines down on Winthrop shore;
The scenes around look lovelier as
  We view them more and more.

Those cottages, so Swiss-like built,
  Geneva's distant banks might deck;
The waters, too, so calmly sweep
  As scarce to cause a wreck.

The numerous birds whose warblings there
  Oft mingle with the gale,

The hourly steamers passing by,
  The yachts which onward sail,

The myriad trees that deck the lawn,
  The flowers that bloom there,
Invite the tired and weary ones
  Just to a spot so fair.

The children's voices scarce we hear,
  For echoes ne'er resound,
Within that blithesome hillside fair,
  Where health and strength are found.

How many from the sunny South
  Do visit it each year!
They leave far-fam'd Virginia,
  To rest in Winthrop fair.

"ASCENSION SOCIETY."

(Founded March, 1887. Boston, 1891.)

———

'Tis formed to aid the good but needy
    Of every nation, race and creed;
Of narrow-minded bigotry
    Its rules they have been freed.

The poor one, and the weak one, too,
    In it will find a home,
And friends to aid them in the strife,
    Wherever they may roam.

Whenever they are homeless, here,
    We feed them part each day,
A lunch is freely given all,
    And none is asked to pay,

Our watchword's like a barrier,
    Which none can force away;
Should females all possess it,
    Not one would ever stray.

Education is a blossom
   Which must bloom on every tree
That the Ascension garden decks,
   Where females enter free.

But hark awhile! the sentinel
   Who always keeps the key
Demands a halt—the password here
   Must proven by you be.

We ask not what your nation is,
   We care not what's your creed,
Your race we ne'er reproach you for,
   But from vices three be freed.

Intemperance locks the outer gate,
   Dishonesty them all;
But fallen female never once
   May tread the Ascension Hall.

Be patient just one moment yet,
   I do not care to vex,
Ascension Hall is not for man,
   But for the nobler sex.

LITTLE GAINS; OR LENTEN PRACTICES.

Let every thought and word and deed
    Be acts of love each day;
Rise early with the morning sun,
    Go rest with its last ray.

Go build a tower to shield thee
    Throughout these weeks of prayer;
Let mortifications deeply felt,
    Be sin's most mighty slayer.

Thy greatest fault keep absent,
    Let none its presence feel;
And moments from thy pleasure
    For prayer be sure you steal.

Thy neighbor's needs forget not,
    Show kindness unto all,

Be gentle to the erring,
    And raise them should they fall.

Should words, unkindly spoken,
    In these days give thee pain,
Go by and do not heed them,
    They'll pass as snow with rain.

To feel not wounds they leave behind
    Is more than man should crave,
For those will aid to deck our crowns
    With gems beyond the grave.

Let thoughts be left unuttered
    Where pride may feel some pain,
As honors lost for virtue's sake
    We surely shall regain.

Let morsels dainty feast thy eyes,
    But coarser meals then choose;
Think often on Mount Sinai's fast,
    For none through penance lose.

If poverty thy lot should be,
  Bear it with patience great ;
Evangelical that virtue is,
  A key to heaven's gate.

With every step and look and act,
  Throughout this season sad,
We can deck our everlasting crown,
  And saints in heaven make glad.

Boston, March, 1895.

www.ingramcontent.com/pod-product-compliance
Lightning Source LLC
Chambersburg PA
CBHW022140020726
47496CB00008B/2484